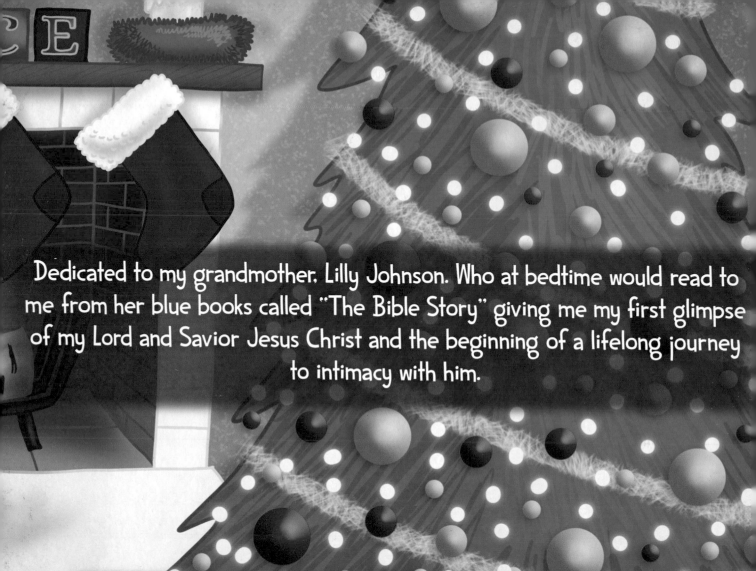

Dedicated to my grandmother, Lilly Johnson. Who at bedtime would read to me from her blue books called "The Bible Story" giving me my first glimpse of my Lord and Savior Jesus Christ and the beginning of a lifelong journey to intimacy with him.

Text copyright © 2019 Greg Huett
Illustrations copyright © 2019 Gideon Burnett
Published in 2019 by Big Country Farm Toys, LLC

ISBN 978-1-7324897-0-7

Printed in China.

The illustrations were created by Gideon Burnett and the story was written by Greg Huett.
Based on the actual farm animals from the Huett family farm.

For more information about Big Country Farm Toys and the Huett family farm, visit www.bigcountrytoys.com

*Special note to parents from the author:

While writing this book I wanted to provide a farm and ranch application to the classic "Twas the Night Before Christmas".

As a follower of Jesus Christ. I couldn't imagine any Christmas book without some mention of the true meaning of the

Christmas holiday. However, as a father of four boys. I understand that this discussion is a very personal matter between

parents and their children. So I tried to include the true meaning but also give you. the parent. the flexibility to discuss the

topic with your child at whatever level is appropriate for your beliefs as well as their age and maturity.

Here are some Bible verses that you might find helpful in your discussions

Luke 2:8

And in the same region there were shepherds out in the field. keeping watch over their

flock by night. And an angel of the Lord appeared to them. and the glory of the Lord

shone around them. and they were filled with great fear. And the angel said to them.

"Fear not for behold. I bring you good news of great joy for all the people.

For unto you is born this day in the city of David a Savior who is Christ the Lord. And this

will be a sign for you: you will find a baby wrapped in swaddling cloths

and lying in a manger."

Romans 3:23

For all have sinned and fall short of the glory of God.

John 3:16

For God so loved the world. that he gave his only son so that whoever believes in him.

shall not perish. but have eternal life.

Christmas is a special time of the year on farmer Jay's farm. The farm and the barn are all decorated for the holidays.

Farmer Jay takes extra special care of all his animals because he loves them and considers them His family.

Farmer Jay and his wife give all the animals a present. A special Christmas treat for each of the farm animals (see the recipe at the back of the book).

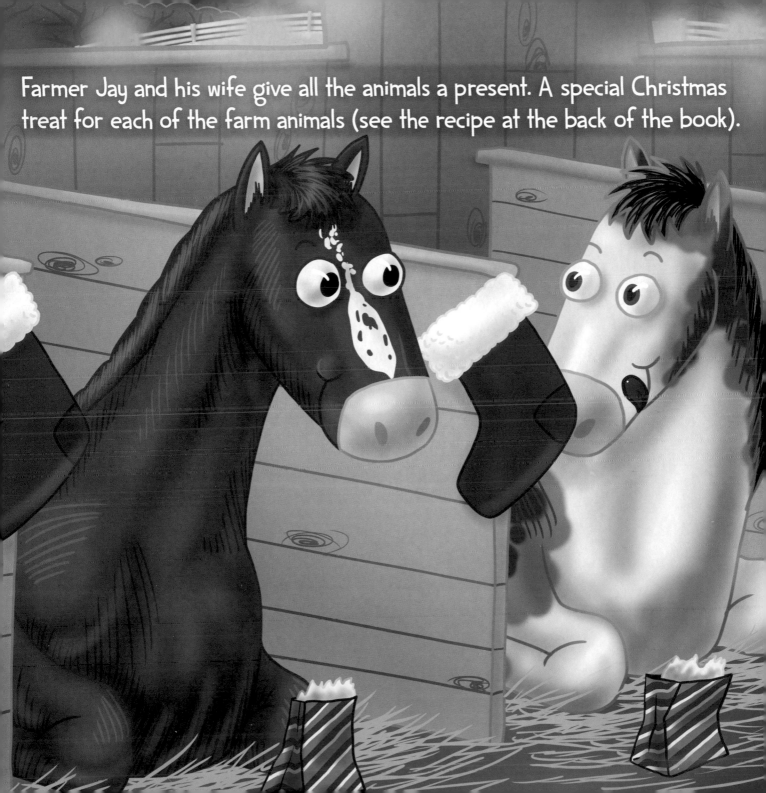

Every year Farmer Jay gathers all the animals on the farm and reads them a Christmas story.

They all gather in the barn where it's nice and warm and the Christmas lights give off a warm glow. And Farmer Jay reads them this story:

PEACE

"'Twas** the night before Christmas,
when all through the house
not a creature was stirring, not even a mouse:
The stockings were hung by the chimney with care,
In hopes that St. Nicholas soon would be there:

The children were nestled all snug in their beds,
While visions of sugar-plums danced in their heads;
And mamma in her 'kerchief, and I in my cap,
Had just settled down for a long winter's nap,

When out on the lawn there arose such a clatter,
I sprang from the bed to see what was the matter.
Away to the window I flew like a flash,
Tore open the shutters and threw up the sash.

The moon on the breast of the new-fallen snow
Gave the luster of mid-day to objects below.
When, what to my wondering eyes should appear,
But a miniature sleigh, and eight tiny reindeer.

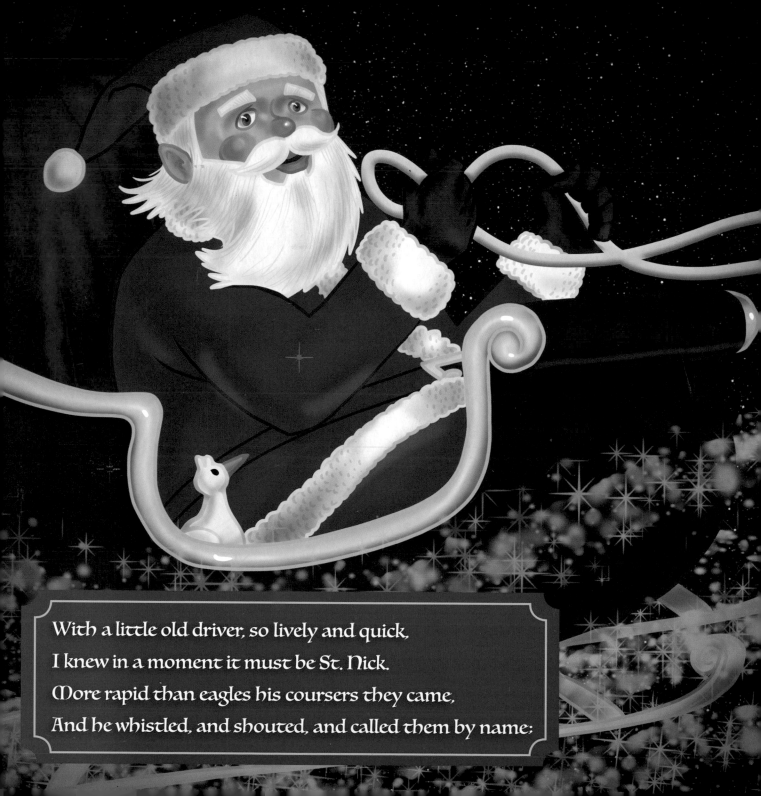

With a little old driver, so lively and quick,

I knew in a moment it must be St. Nick.

More rapid than eagles his coursers they came,

And he whistled, and shouted, and called them by name:

"Now, DASHER! now, DANCER!
now, PRANCER and VIXEN!
On, COMET! on CUPID!
on, DONNER and BLITZEN!

"To the top of the porch! to the top of the wall!

Now dash away! dash away! dash away all!"

As dry leaves that before the wild hurricane fly,

When they meet with an obstacle, mount to the sky,

So up to the house-top the coursers they flew,
With the sleigh full of toys, and St. Nicholas too.
And then, in a twinkling, I heard on the roof
The prancing and pawing of each little hoof.

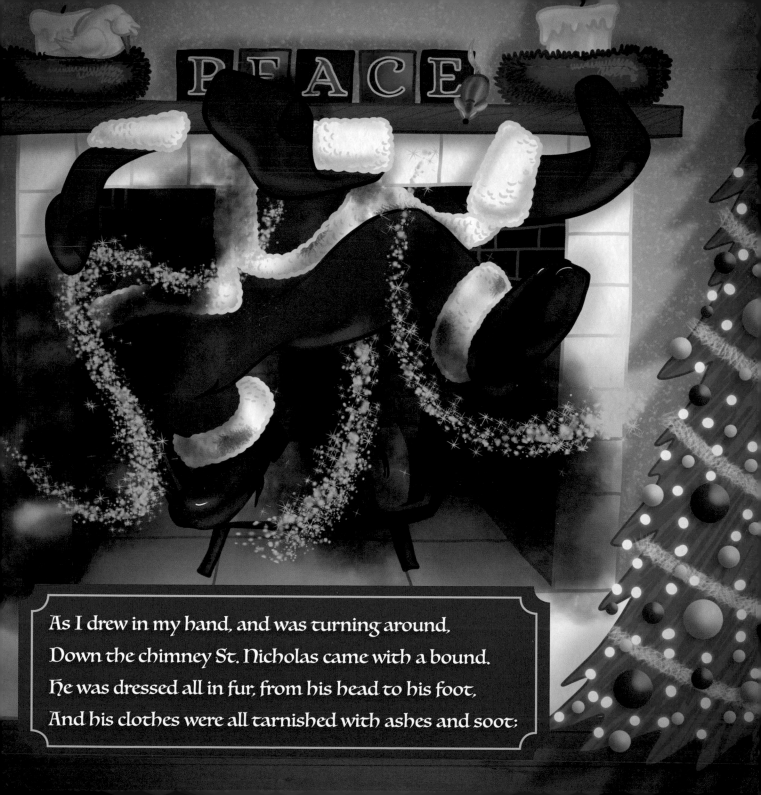

As I drew in my hand, and was turning around,
Down the chimney St. Nicholas came with a bound.
He was dressed all in fur, from his head to his foot,
And his clothes were all tarnished with ashes and soot:

A bundle of toys he had flung on his back,
And he looked like a peddler just opening his pack.
His eyes— how they twinkled! his dimples how merry!
His cheeks were like roses, his nose like a cherry!

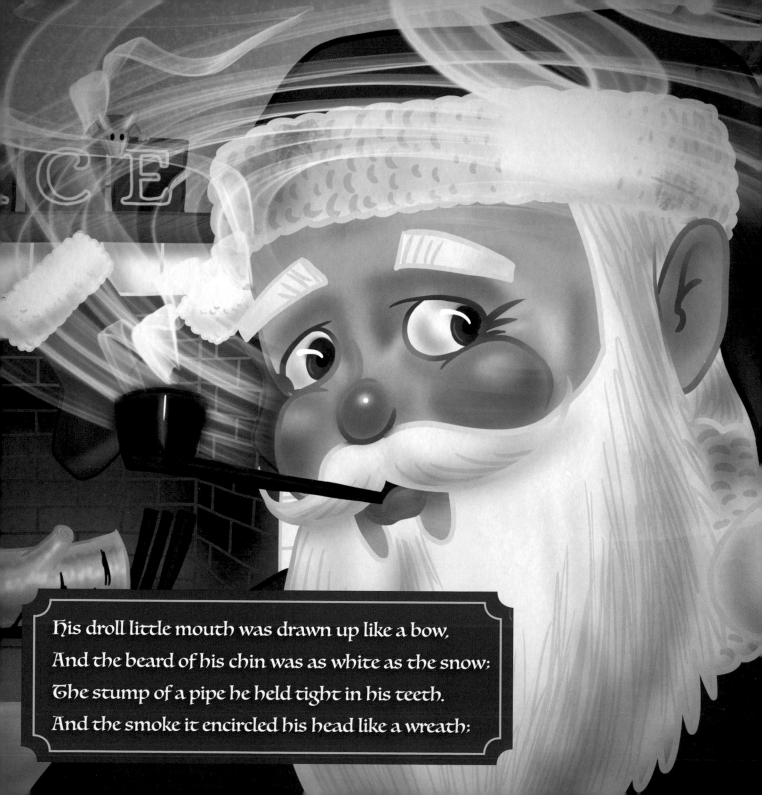

His droll little mouth was drawn up like a bow,
And the beard of his chin was as white as the snow;
The stump of a pipe he held tight in his teeth,
And the smoke it encircled his head like a wreath;

He had a broad face and a little round belly,
That shook when he laughed like a bowlful of jelly.
He was chubby and plump, a right jolly old elf,
And I laughed when I saw him, in spite of myself:

A wink of his eye and a twist of his head,

Soon gave me to know I had nothing to dread;

He spoke not a word, but went straight to his work,

And filled all the stockings; then turned with a jerk,

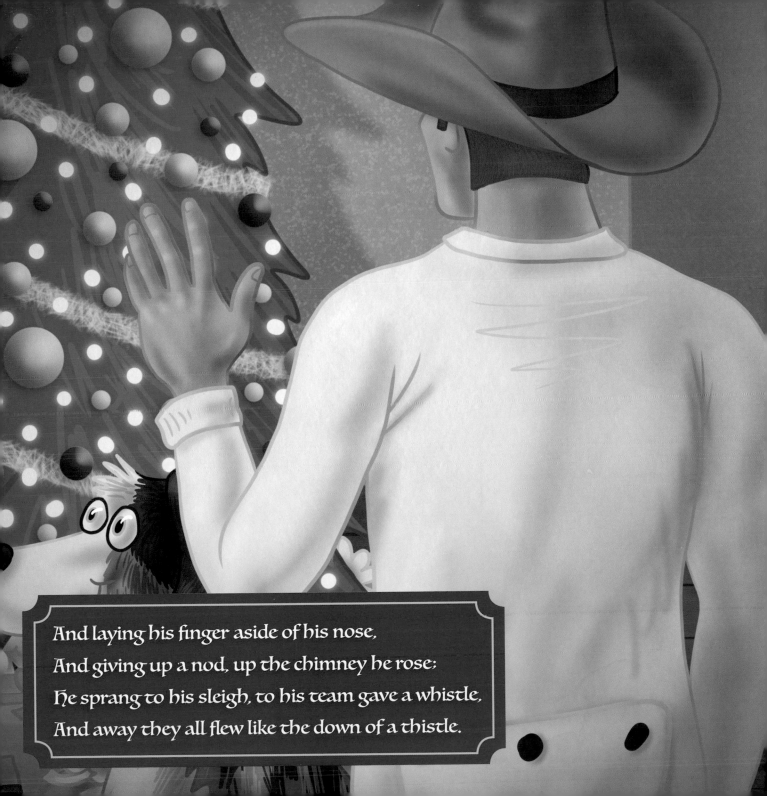

And laying his finger aside of his nose,

And giving up a nod, up the chimney he rose:

He sprang to his sleigh, to his team gave a whistle,

And away they all flew like the down of a thistle.

But I heard him exclaim, ere he drove out of sight,
HAPPY CHRISTMAS TO ALL, AND TO ALL A GOOD-NIGHT!

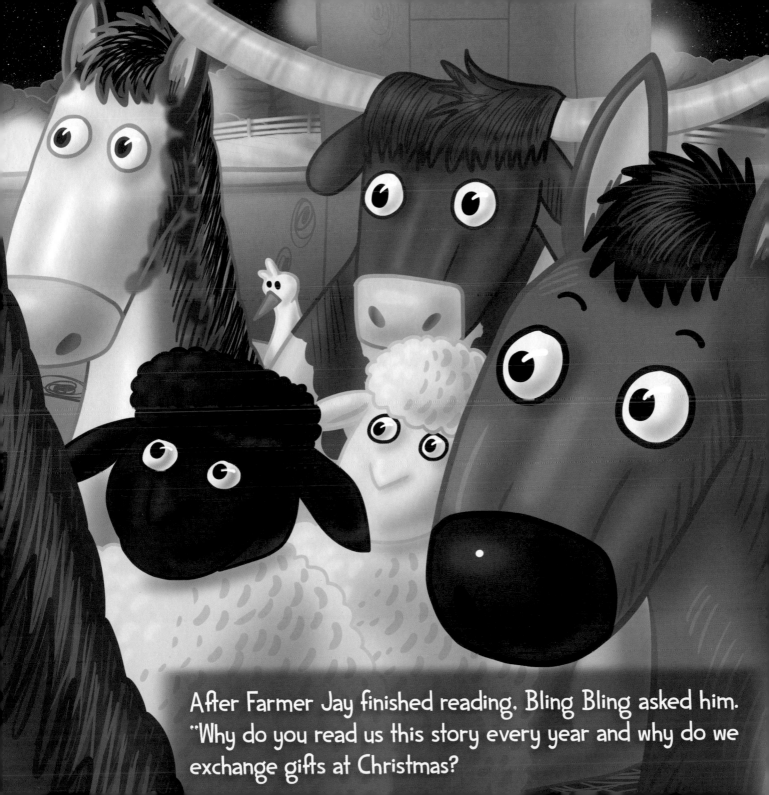

After Farmer Jay finished reading, Bling Bling asked him. "Why do you read us this story every year and why do we exchange gifts at Christmas?

Farmer Jay gathered all the animals around him, asked them to sit down and began to explain the true meaning of Christmas.

He told them, "We celebrate Christmas and exchange gifts in celebration of an actual event that happened over 2,000 years ago. Christmas is a birthday celebration for Jesus Christ. That is why it is called Christ-Mas.

The gifts represent two things:
First, there were actually three wise men who brought
the baby Jesus gifts of gold, frankincense and myrrh.

And the gifts represent the purpose of the baby Jesus. He was a gift to all of us. And through his life we can receive the greatest gift of all. So every year we get together and exchange gifts to remind us of his love for us.

That night all the animals understood why Farmer Jay loved Christmas and why they exchange gifts. And all the animals were so thankful to be a part of Farmer Jay's farm.

Barnyard Cookie Recipe

Treat your barnyard animals to tasty cookies this holiday season (great for horses. cows. goats. dogs and pigs). Animals love treats and you can make your own with just a few ingredients your mom or dad have on hand. What better gift to give your barnyard animals than their own special holiday cookies?

Ingredients:

4 cups grain (we use oats)

8 tablespoons of flour

1/2 cup of molasses

3/4 cup of water

Yields about 36 cookies.

Instructions:

Step 1: Combine all ingredients in a large mixing bowl. Stir with a large spoon until the mixture is the consistency of thick cookie dough.

Step 2: Drop tablespoons of dough on a greased cookie sheet. spacing cookies 1 inch apart.

Step 3: Drizzle molasses on top of each cookie with a spoon.

Step 4: Bake at 300 degrees Fahrenheit for 1 hour or until crisp. Remove from oven and cool for 30 minutes.

Step 5: Place cookies in decorative gift bags.

Bling

We hope you have enjoyed Christmas on the Farm. For some extra fun, go back and try to find the doves we have placed along the way, in various places in the story. You should be able to find all 21. You can find additional books along with farm, ranch and rodeo toys on our website at www.bigcountrytoys.com.

Check out some of the actual farm animal characters living on the Huett farm:

Woodrow stuck in the hay ring

Bling

Lucy

Clovie Jean and Hayden

Scan this QR code to learn more about the Huett Farm and their animals

Ellie

Greg and Bling

Baby Woodrow

Big Sway

Woodrow stuck in the hay ring

Woodrow

Laurie Darling

Scan this QR code to learn more
about the Huett Farm and their animals

Minnie Ruth

Benny

Big Red

Scarlet

Bud Bud and Hayden

Bud Bud

Timmy

Scan this QR code to learn more
about the Huett Farm and their animals